BL 2.1 AR 0.5 = 1/2 pt

3/01

WHAT A BAD DREAM

BY MERCER MAYER

For Amy & Shelton

MATTESON PUBLIC LIBRARY

A GOLDEN BOOK • NEW YORK

Golden Books Publishing Company, Inc., New York, New York 10106

I had a dream that I made a magic potion.
After I mixed it up, I drank the potion down.

Then weird things started to happen,
just like in a spooky show on television.

I changed.
I grew pointy fangs

and long claws.

I had bat wings and a long tail.

I could roar so loud that I scared everybody,
and they left me alone.
Then I did whatever I wanted.

I lived all by myself.
My room looked just the way I wanted it to look.

I had cookies and ice cream for breakfast.

I never brushed my fur or my fangs,
and I never changed my clothes.

I got a gorilla for a pet.

I didn't go to school.
I just rode my bicycle
wherever I wanted.

We ate ice cream and fudge pops for lunch.

We played outside as long as we wanted—
even after it was dark.

At dinnertime we just
ordered in pizza
and didn't use napkins.

I never took a bath—even if I was dirty.
I kept lizards and frogs and snakes in the tub.

I watched television as late as I wanted
and never even had to go to bed.

I got sleepy anyway and went upstairs.
But there was no one to tuck me in
and read me a story.

Then I got scared, and there was no one
to give me a hug. I began to cry.
I wanted my mommy and daddy.

Suddenly someone was shaking me.
It was my mom and dad.
"You had a bad dream," they said.

"Time to put you in bed," said Dad.
"That's not a magic potion, is it?" I asked.

"No, it's just warm milk," said Mom.
"Good," I said. "I don't want a magic potion."